COUNT

COUNT

MELVIN BURGESS

ILLUSTRATED BY CHRIS MOULD

ANDERSEN PRESS

First published in 2021 by
Andersen Press Limited
20 Vauxhall Bridge Road, London, SW1V 2SA, UK
Vijverlaan 48, 3062 HL Rotterdam, Nederland
www.andersenpress.co.uk

2 4 6 8 10 9 7 5 3 1

British Library Cataloguing in Publication Data available.

ISBN 978 1 78344 988 0

Printed and bound in Great Britain by
Clays Ltd, Elcograf S.p.A.

For Beckon and Rebecca Simpson – M.B.

1

Brandon Wright is the **best** footballer. He'd show you if it wasn't for that toe injury that's kept him out of action for the past few months.

And he's the **strongest** in his class. When he bends his arm, his muscles stick up in the air like rocks underneath that baggy jumper he always wears. You could feel them for yourself, but he won't let you because he's so tickly. Brandon is so tickly, all you have to do is look at him and he starts to squirm.

And he's the best at maths and at singing and at drawing, and he has the best bike and the fastest skates and the best mum . . .

In fact, if you listen to Brandon, he's the best at **everything.**

No one believes any of it of course, but Brandon doesn't mind. He's not good at much really – not good at football or maths or drawing or singing. There's just one thing everyone knows he's the best at.

Boasting. Brandon is the best boaster in the school. 'What an imagination!' said his teacher Mr Wyke once. 'But you know, Brandon, you can't pretend *all* the time. No one will believe a word you say!'

It wasn't true that no one believed him. His little sister Elle believed every single word that came out of his mouth. She was the only one in the whole wide world who did.

2

Someone was boasting in the playground but for once, it wasn't Brandon. It was Brandon's best friend, Waris. Last night in bed, before he went to sleep, Waris had counted all the way up to **one thousand**.

He'd been trying to do it all week, but he kept getting mixed up and missing numbers out. Not this time. This time he got all the way there. His dad lay on his bed and checked to make sure he got it right.

561
560
559
558
557
556
555

'It took me half an hour,' said Waris. 'I had to be very careful not to fall asleep. My dad did, twice. I had to wake him up by shouting the numbers at him.'

'I counted up to six hundred once,' said Sophie, 'but then my mum said it was time to stop.'

'I tried too, but I got bored,' said Mu.

'I bet you could count higher than that, Brandon, couldn't you?' said Elle.

'Easy,' said Brandon. But he said it quietly, because Waris was his friend and he'd lost a lot of friends lately because of boasting too much.

'How high could you go, Brandon?'

'TEN MILLION,' said Brandon, without even thinking.

'Do it now,' said Elle. 'Go on. Please, Brandon.'

'Now's not a good time.'

'Please?'

Brandon knew the bell would go any time soon, and he thought he'd have to stop then. So he took Elle quietly away to a corner and began to count in a low voice, so that no one else could hear.

'One, two, three, four, five, six, seven,' he said.

'Go, Brandon,' said Elle.

'Eight, nine, ten, eleven,' said Brandon – still very quietly.

'HEY, EVERYONE!' shouted Elle suddenly, at the top of her very loud voice. 'Look at Brandon. He's counting all the way up to TEN MILLION!'

Brandon blushed bright red, but he didn't stop counting. He scowled at Elle, dug his hands deep in his pockets and marched away.

'Twenty-one, twenty-two, twenty-three, twenty-four!' he said angrily.

'Sorry, Brandon,' said Elle. But it was too late. Everyone had left Waris and they were following Brandon to listen to him count up to **TEN MILLION**.

Waris was furious.

'No one can count up to **TEN MILLION**,' he said. 'It's another stupid Brandon boast.'

'Thirty-two, thirty-three, thirty-four, thirty-five,' muttered Brandon in a sorry kind of voice. He waved his hands at everyone to make them go back to Waris. But he didn't stop counting.

'forty-one, forty-two,

'You *always* do this,' said Waris. 'Every time someone does something, you ruin it by boasting how much better you could do it – and then you *never* do. Well, this time, I'm going to make sure. I'm going to stay right next to you and listen to you count all the way up to TEN MILLION.'

Brandon shook his head, but Waris took no notice.

forty-three, forty-four, forty-five.'

'Hey, everyone!' he shouted. 'Come and listen to Brandon count up to TEN MILLION!'

All around the playground, people gathered to listen to the great event.

'fifty, fifty-one, fifty-two,' groaned Brandon. There was no way he could back down now. And he wasn't even up to one hundred yet. This could take for ever!

Then the bell went.

In the classroom, Mr Wyke was drawing a picture of a Viking longship on the board. The class were writing in their books about Vikings.

'Who's talking?' asked Mr Wyke suddenly.

He paused in his drawing. 'No talking, please,' he said. He carried on for a moment, but he could still hear talking. He turned round.

'Someone is *still* talking,' he said. He looked around the class. Everyone had their heads down writing, but someone was talking, all right.

'Whoever it is, you can stop it right now,' said Mr Wyke, angrily. Who could it be?

Waris jumped up.

'It's Brandon, sir,' he said.

'Brandon?' said Mr Wyke. Brandon kept his face down. Mr Wyke walked closer to listen. Yes – it *was* Brandon. He was muttering to himself.

'He's counting, sir,' said Waris.

'Counting? In a history lesson?'

'Up to **TEN MILLION**, sir.'

'Brandon – is this true?'

'859, 860, 861, 862, 863,' said Brandon.

He sat up and glared angrily at Waris, who folded his arms and put his nose in the air.

Mr Wyke listened to Brandon for a moment. It was very good counting. Beautiful, even. But this was a history lesson. You can't have counting in a history lesson!

'I'd like you to stop it now, Brandon,' he said firmly. 'We'll be doing some maths this afternoon. You can count then.'

'919, 920, 921,' said Brandon stubbornly.

'Stop him before he gets to a thousand,' said Waris excitedly.

'923, 924, 925,' sneered Brandon.

'Stop it, Brandon – right now, if you please,' said Mr Wyke.

'927, 928, 929,' said Brandon, looking sideways at Waris.

'I said, stop!' snapped Mr Wyke.

'930,' said Brandon.

'Right! Out of my classroom right now. Go and stand in the corridor,' roared Mr Wyke.

Brandon got to his feet and slouched towards the door. '941,' he said.

He left the room.

'Counting in a history lesson! Ridiculous,' said Mr Wyke.

'I bet he's still at it out there,' said Waris.

'You can be quiet too, Waris,' said Mr Wyke. He got back to drawing his Viking ship, but a couple of minutes later, the class door opened and Brandon popped his head inside.

'ONE THOUSAND!'

'I don't care,' Waris
roared back.

'Silence!' bellowed
Mr Wyke.

'1,001,' said Brandon.

And he closed the door.

Brandon stood outside the classroom counting for the rest of the lesson. He counted all the way through lunch, too. After that it was a maths lesson so Mr Wyke let him back in the class. But he was still counting out loud while he was supposed to be doing sums quietly, so he got sent out again.

By this time, the news of Brandon's counting was all over the school. Even Miss Hexx the headteacher had heard about it.

Miss Hexx was an expert headteacher. The school had done rather badly before under the old head, so it had been put into 'special measures' and the most special of those special measures was Miss Hexx herself. She was very strict and had a list of rules all aimed at making good schools out of bad. *Silence in class* was one of them. And absolutely *no getting sent outside* was another.

So when Brandon saw her walking down the corridor towards him, dressed in her sparkly blue business suit, he knew he was in trouble.

But instead of telling him off she broke into a big smile.

7,558

7,557

7,556

'Brandon Wright!' she said. 'I never knew you were so good at counting. Where are you up to now?'

'7,559,' said Brandon.

'What? Really?'

'7,560, 7,561,' said Brandon.

'Wow. That's quite something,' said Miss Hexx. But she was still going to stop him. You couldn't have people doing great things in school just when they felt like it. Miss Hexx wanted results – exam results. No one ever got good exam results by counting.

'That's great!' she said cunningly. 'It's a school record. I'm going to have a certificate made and put it up on the wall. What a good job Mr Wyke has done teaching you your numbers. Come on – let's stop now and go back inside and tell everyone how well you've done.'

But Brandon had been counting for over

four hours and he wasn't going to stop now. He had made up his mind. For once in his life, this wasn't a boast. Even though Miss Hexx scared him silly, he was still going to count all the way up to TEN MILLION.

He tucked his hands under his arms and shook his head. '7,577, 7,578,' he said firmly. '7,579.'

'Brandon,' said Miss Hexx dangerously. 'Stop counting and let's go.'

'7,580,' said Brandon. '7,581, 7,582.'

'Don't you dare disobey me! I'm your headteacher!' said Miss Hexx.

Brandon was so scared he shook in his shoes, but all he said was: '7,583.'

'You ridiculous and stubborn child!' exclaimed Miss Hexx. 'Just counting away whenever you feel like it, without a thought for anyone else. We'll see about that. I'm calling an SSM – a Special School Meeting – about you, Brandon Wright. And I shall be speaking to your parents.'

She turned her back and walked away. Behind her, Brandon slid down the wall to the floor. He put his face in his hands.

The last time someone had an SSM called about them, they left school and were never seen again. Now he really was in trouble.

'Brandon!' snapped Miss Hexx suddenly from the end of the corridor. 'Stand up!'

Brandon jumped to his feet.

'And stop counting this instant!'

'7,591,' he said firmly.

'YOU JUST WAIT!' shouted Miss Hexx. She went back into her office and slammed the door. She'd never seen such disobedience in her whole life.

Miss Hexx was so cross she called all the teachers in for an SSM that very day.

'We can't have it,' she said. 'School is for lessons. Things have to be learned in the right order, at the right time and in the right way. You can't have children doing things just because they're good at them.'

Mr Wyke sighed. 'I suppose so,' he said. 'It is a pity though.'

'A pity?' said Miss Hexx. 'What are you on about, Mr Wyke?'

'It's the way he does it,' murmured Mr Wyke '. . . the way the numbers just keep going up and up. One after the other. Time after time. It's . . . well. It's rather *beautiful*.'

A lot of the other teachers had stopped off over the day to listen to the boy who wouldn't stop counting. Some of them, the ones who loved numbers, smiled to themselves as they thought about just how lovely Brandon's counting was.

'That's just the sort of attitude that brought this school into special measures,' snapped Miss Hexx. 'Beauty is not a curriculum subject. It passes no exams and it cannot be measured. If Brandon wants to be beautiful, he can do it in his own time. He *must be stopped*.'

Mr Wyke nodded sadly. 'I suppose so,' he said. 'In that case, I have an idea that may just do it.'

It was the last lesson of the day and Brandon was back in the classroom. Miss Hexx was there too. Everyone was on their best behaviour.

'Right,' said Mr Wyke. 'Counting up to TEN MILLION. How long will it take? Hands up!'

Some people thought it would take days. Some thought weeks. One boy said it would take two months.

'Let's do the maths,' said Mr Wyke, scribbling numbers on the board. 'Brandon counts one number every two seconds . . .' *scribble scribble scribble* . . . 'But once he gets onto the longer numbers it's going to take more like three seconds . . .' *scribble scribble* . . . 'In one hour . . .' *scribble scribble* . . . 'he counts 1,200 numbers. In a day, he can count 28,800. So to count to TEN MILLION, it's going to take him about . . .' *scribble scribble scribble scribble scribble* . . .

'Just a few weeks short of

ONE WHOLE YEAR!'

The whole class gasped.

'With no sleep,' said Mr Wyke.

He turned around to look at Brandon. Brandon's jaw was hanging open.

'It's now early October. Brandon's going to be counting up to next September *at least*.'

'Yes!' said the headteacher, leaping up at the back of the class. 'And if he continues this ridiculous nonsense, I'm going to exclude him from school, so his mum won't be able to go to work. How about that, Brandon, eh? So you're not just going to be bored with counting for months and months. You're going to be *poor* as well.

'Your whole family will get poorer and poorer the longer you count. When Christmas comes, the rest of us will be having fun with our *expensive* presents and stuffing our faces with *delicious* food, but you, Brandon Wright, will be getting no presents at all. *Your* family will be huddled up eating cold baked beans because that's all you'll be able to afford.

'And why? Because of one thing – counting!'

She marched smartly to the door. 'Happy counting, Brandon,' she said with a smirk. 'See you tomorrow – without any numbers *if* you don't mind.'

And she closed the door with a bang. The class listened in silence to her heels clacking away on the floor.

Brandon had gone as white as a sheet. '10,251,' he groaned.

Mr Wyke pulled a face. 'I'm sorry, Brandon,' he said. 'You count better than anyone else I've ever heard. But it has to stop. You can see that, can't you? This is a *school*. You're supposed to *learn* how to do things – you're not supposed to actually start *doing* them yourself until you're grown up.'

Brandon shook his head. A tear ran down his face. '10,255,' he wept. A whole year! He'd never dreamed it was going to take that long.

What about Christmas? What about his sister, Elle? He couldn't do that to her – could he? And what was his mum going to say about all this?

'See?' said Waris, leaning across and nudging him in the ribs. 'That'll teach you to boast.'

After school, Waris walked home with Brandon and Elle.

'I know you're cheating,' said Waris. 'No one can count that high.'

'12,050,' said Brandon smugly.

'You're missing out numbers, I expect,' said Waris. 'Well, you can fool everyone else but you can't fool me. I'm glued to your side until I spot you cheating or messing up.'

'Brandon doesn't cheat,' said Elle. 'Everything he ever says is true.'

'Yeah right, and pigs fly south for the winter,' said Waris. They carried on walking. 'Anyway,' he said, 'what's your mum going to say when she finds out?'

'12,071, 12,072,' said Brandon miserably. He had a letter in his pocket from Miss Hexx to his mother. He knew what that was going to be about.

When they got home, Waris marched in and told Brandon's mum that Brandon had asked him to tea.

'Is that right, Brandon?' asked his mum.

'12,703,' said Brandon, glaring at Waris.

'What?' said his mum.

'He's counting,' said Waris. 'All the way up to TEN MILLION – if you believe him, that is. Which no one does. It's going to take him nearly a year. With no sleep. He has a letter about it from Miss Hexx in his pocket for you.'

'12,707,' said Brandon sadly. He put his

hand in his pocket and pulled out the letter for his mum.

'I'm here to check up and make sure he misses none of the numbers out,' said Waris.

'I see.' Mum fixed them all up with drinks and sandwiches at the table, and read the letter.

Todley Junior School
Et utile vel relinquo

Dear Mrs Wright,

I am sorry to tell you that Brandon has been extremely difficult today. He won't stop counting, even when asked very nicely. As a result he is falling behind in his school work.

This must stop! The modern school has no place for individualistic achievement and unregulated counting. When he comes back to school tomorrow I expect him to have stopped. If not, I shall have no choice but to send him straight back home.

Yours sincerely,
Miss Delia Hexx (Headteacher)

Mum looked over to where the children were eating their sandwiches. Elle was looking at Brandon in adoration. Waris had his ear as close to Brandon's mouth as he could get it. And Brandon? Brandon was counting.

'Brandon,' said Mum. 'Don't talk with your mouth full.'

'12,823,' said Brandon through a mouthful of partially chewed cheese sandwich.

'Brandon!' snapped Mum.

'12,824,' said Brandon defiantly, and he took a big bite of sandwich. '12,825,' he added, spitting cheese sandwich over Waris's ear.

Mum closed her eyes and counted to ten herself.

'Did you hear that, Mum?' said Elle. '12,825! Brandon is the Counting King, isn't he, Mum?'

'He's the Cheating King,' said Waris.

'Waris can only count up to One thousand,' said Elle.

'It's going to take him a year!' shouted Waris.

'Be quiet all of you. I'm trying to think,' said Mum.

There were a number of things Brandon's mum could have done. She could have got angry and sent Brandon to bed, or stopped his pocket money, or not let him go swimming in the week.

But . . .

'MUM, MUM . . .'

'Not now, Elle.'

'But look, Mum. Look at Brandon counting.'

Mum turned to look. Brandon was sitting at the table, his face raised up towards the light coming through the window. The numbers seemed to be flowing out of him in perfect order, one after the other. But the really wonderful thing was how beautiful each number was on Brandon's lips. How strange, thought Mum, that she'd never noticed how lovely numbers were before now.

'Brandon,' she whispered.

Brandon didn't seem to hear. He gazed out towards the window, the light shining on his face. Next to him, Waris was watching him too, mouth open, eyes wide, as if he were watching something so much more than just a boy counting, like a sunset, or a flock of swans flying over a lake at dawn.

'Brandon,' said Mum, loudly. Brandon shook his head and sank back into his chair.

'13,357,' he muttered grumpily.

'. . . Must be cheating,' grumbled Waris.

'Can we watch TV?' asked Elle.

'13,361,' said Brandon.

Mum made up her mind. Brandon had never done anything much in his life except boast, and now he was doing something extraordinary. She'd never heard of anyone counting so high or so beautifully. Perhaps he was cheating, like Waris said, because who ever heard of an eight-year-old boy counting up to thirteen thousand and beyond? Even so, she didn't want to be the one to make him stop.

Anyway, she thought . . . bedtime was only a few hours away. No one, no matter how good they were, could count in their sleep. In the morning it would all be forgotten about, Brandon could go to school, she could go to work, and everything would be back to normal.

Right through the evening, through dinner and after-dinner games time, Waris stayed as close to Brandon as he could, listening to him count.

At eight o'clock, Waris's mum, Anandi, came to take him back home. While Mum was answering the door, Waris stood up, sighed, and looked down at his friend.

'It's true, isn't it?' he said. 'You really have counted all the way up to . . .'

'**16,637**,' said Brandon.

'. . . and you haven't missed out a single number.' Waris shook his head in wonder.

'Brandon, I never thought I'd say this, but that's pretty amazing. You are the Counting King, like Elle said. I'm sorry I doubted you.'

He put out his hand, and Brandon jumped up, grabbed hold of it and gave it a big, hard shake.

'16,641!' he said happily.

16,642

16,643

The two boys stood and beamed at one another for a moment, before Mum came back in with Waris's mum. Waris said goodnight . . .

'And good luck!' he added.

'16,647,' said Brandon proudly.

Yes! He really was the Counting King.

9

Bedtime came.

'Goodnight, Elle. Goodnight, Brandon,' said Mum.

'Goodnight, Mum,' said Elle.

'17,217,' said Brandon.

Mum tiptoed out and closed the bedroom door. Then, on second thoughts, she opened the door an inch, so that she could hear Brandon counting. She told herself she did this just to check that he'd fall asleep and finally stop, but secretly . . . secretly she loved listening to her son count. There was something so peaceful about it, it made her want to fall quietly asleep herself.

'17,229,' murmured Brandon in a drowsy voice.

So beautiful, she thought. Brandon was bound to stop when he fell asleep – any minute now, judging by how tired his voice sounded. It was a shame it had to end, but a good thing too.

Feeling tired herself, Mum went to lie on her own bed for a moment before she went downstairs to do a few last chores. But as she lay listening to Brandon's musical counting in the room next door, the numbers lulled her gently into a land of beautiful dreams.

She woke up hours later, still lying on her bed fully clothed. Elle was standing next to her.

'What is it, Elle?'

'Come and see Brandon counting, Mum.'

Mum glanced at the clock. It was half-past two in the morning. And . . . Brandon was still counting? It couldn't be!

And yet, as she left her bedroom and walked the few steps across the landing to Brandon's room, she saw that it was so. She could hear his murmuring voice naming the numbers one after the other. From inside the room, even though the light was off, a shimmering gold and silver light was casting mysterious patterns on the walls.

She pushed open the door. Brandon lay in bed, eyes closed, fast asleep . . . but his lips were still moving.

23,021
23,022

'23,023, 23,024,' he whispered to the pillow. 23,025,
23,026,
23,027, 23,028, 23,029,
23,030.'

'Oh my Lord,' said Mum. Brandon was still counting even *in his sleep!* All around him, out of the corner of her eyes, she could see dancing lights. They hung in the air around her son, some gold, some silver, some blue, some red, shimmering and dancing in the gloom of the bedroom, like magical beings come from the spirit world to visit for a night.

'It's the numbers, Mum,' said Elle. 'They've come for Brandon to count them.

They're waiting for their turn.'

Numbers, come to be counted? Surely it wasn't possible! And yet, when she screwed up her eyes and tilted her head and looked sideways, she could see that, yes, those lights were numbers, hundreds and thousands of numbers. Millions of them. They spiralled around the room and out of the window.

23,565, 23,566, 23,567, 23,568, 23,569, 23,570, 23,571, 23,572, 23,573, 23,574, 23,575, 23,576, 23,577, 23,578, 23,579, 23,580, 23,581, 23,582, 23,583, 23,584, 23,585, 23,586, 23,587, 23,588, 23,589, 23,590, 23,591, 23,592, 23,593, 23,594, 23,595, 23,596, 23,597, 23,598, 23,599, 23,600, 23,601,

She could see them queueing patiently all the way to the moon and back, waiting for their turn for Brandon to give them their names.

'It can't be,' she whispered.

But it was.

'The numbers love Brandon, don't they, Mum?' said Elle.

As usual, Elle was right. The numbers did love Brandon. And Brandon loved the numbers right back.

10

Waris always set his alarm for seven every morning. He needed the extra time to go online and play *Fortnite*. But today he woke up suddenly at seven with a big idea.

He knew Brandon wouldn't be up yet so he spent an hour online, doing research before he got onto his laptop and sent a message.

Still counting?

There was an anxious wait of a few minutes before the answer came back . . .

29,761

Waris gasped and ran into the kitchen.

'He's speeded up in the night, Mum,' he

shouted. 'We have to get round there, quick, before he gets to thirty thousand!'

'Why?' asked Anandi. But Waris was already halfway down the hall, so she grabbed his anorak and hat and ran after him.

It was a blowy day, with puddles on the ground and rain in the air. They were out of breath and wet through by the time they arrived.

Waris hammered at the door, which was opened by Brandon's mum, looking puzzled.

'Where is he?' yelled Waris.

'In the bathroom,' said Mum. Waris darted under her arm and bounded up the stairs like a polecat. Mum looked at Anandi, who smiled and shrugged.

'You know what he's like,' she said.

Waris was on the landing now, banging on the bathroom door. 'Brandon! Let me in!'

Inside Brandon was doing his teeth. '29,993?' he said in a blurry kind of way. '29,994?'

'Brandon! Now! Quick!' roared Waris.

A couple of seconds later the door opened.

Brandon stood there in his pyjama bottoms, with a toothbrush in his mouth.

'29,995?' he asked, but you could hardly make it out because of the brush and the toothpaste.

'Brandon!' howled Waris. He shoved him over to the basin and forced his head into the bowl . . . 'Spit!' he yelled.

Brandon spat.

Waris pulled him back up, wiped his mouth on the flannel and pushed him up against the wall. He had his mum's phone in his hand. 'Count. Clearly now,' he said.

'**29,998?**' said Brandon, frowning. What was going on?

'Go on,' said Waris, filming Brandon as he counted.

'**29,999**,' said Brandon.

'Yessss!' whispered Waris to himself.

'**30,000**,' said Brandon.

'**YES!**' roared Waris. '**Yes, yes, yes!** That's going up on YouTube right now. Brandon, you're going to be an **Internet counting sensation**. And I'm going to be your manager.'

By the time Mum and Anandi were ready to drop off the kids at school, Brandon was up to . . .

'31,847,' he said happily.

Mum looked at him anxiously. The letter from Miss Hexx had said he wasn't to come back unless he'd stopped counting.

'Oh, don't worry so much,' said Anandi. 'They can't send him home for being good at something. Brandon's practically a genius.'

Mum wasn't so sure. She smuggled Brandon in without Miss Hexx seeing him and had a word with Mr Wyke about it.

'I just can't afford to take a day off work,' she whispered. 'You know how it is.'

Mr Wyke did know how it was. Brandon's family was very poor. They lived in a tiny damp house and Mum worked long hours to keep a roof over their heads.

'I'll do my best to hide him from Miss Hexx,' he said. 'But you do realise it has to stop, don't you?'

'Just until I find out how,' whispered Mum.

During lessons, Mr Wyke, who had always loved maths, made Brandon sit at the front of the class. He was amazed that anyone could count so high of course. But the main thing was, he could not understand why it was so lovely to listen to.

33,497, 33,498, 33,499, 33,500, 33,501, 33,502, 33,503, 33,504,

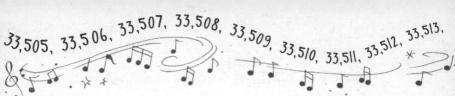

33,505, 33,506, 33,507, 33,508, 33,509, 33,510, 33,511, 33,512, 33,513,

'Like music,' he whispered to himself. 'Like the most beautiful music I've ever heard.'

The counting was so lovely that sometimes he forgot he was supposed to be teaching. At such moments, the air seemed to shimmer and Brandon glowed with a mysterious golden light.

Brandon's counting enchanted not only Mr Wyke, but quite a few of the students as well. Soon, Waris, Natalie, Mu, Amber, David, Sam, Ollie and Pearl were all sitting at their desks, mouths wide open, listening to the numbers flowing out of his mouth like songs.

33,514, 33,515, 33,516, 33,517, 33,518, 33,519, 33,520, 33,521, 33,522,

The rest of the class were bored silly.

Maybe they couldn't see the numbers shining on the air. Maybe they couldn't hear how wonderfully Brandon counted. Maybe they just didn't like numbers – who knows? Anyway, they weren't sitting quietly and listening – they were talking, laughing, running up and down in between the desks, shouting, making paper aeroplanes, yelling, making a fuss and getting into fights.

And Mr Wyke was under such a spell that he didn't even notice.

It couldn't last. It didn't last. Just before break, Miss Hexx was walking down the corridor when she heard a dreadful racket coming out of Mr Wyke's class. She opened the door. Inside she saw a sight to give any headteacher nightmares. Children running when they should be sitting, shouting when they should be being quiet, playing when they should be working.

'SILENCE!' she bellowed.

Mr Wyke nearly fell off his chair in shock. The children who had been under Brandon's spell jumped half a metre into the air. Everyone else ran back to their seats. The only one who took no notice of her was Brandon himself. He stood at the front of the room with his arms slightly raised, chanting out the numbers as if they were some sort of spell or prayer.

'35,897,' he sang. '35,898, 35,899.'

'BRANDON WRIGHT!' roared Miss Hexx. 'STOP THAT THIS INSTANT!'

Brandon shook his head and looked around. Seeing Miss Hexx for the first time, he scowled and crept back to his seat, muttering numbers to himself. He sat down, folded his arms and looked crossly at the headteacher.

'Counting in class,' hissed Miss Hexx. 'Stopping others from learning. Disruptive behaviour. Where will it end? Out. NOW!' she bawled. Brandon pulled a face but did as he was told. He got out of his chair and slouched to the door.

'35,917,' he said.

'Children like you don't deserve school,' hissed Miss Hexx. 'As for you, Mr Wyke – see me after class. I won't tolerate disobedience from my teachers either.'

She stamped out and slammed the door. Outside, everyone heard Brandon saying . . .

'35,923.'

'ARRRRGHGHGHGH!' screamed Miss Hexx.

'Poor Brandon,' said Mr Wyke.

'What will she do to him?' asked Waris.

But Mr Wyke shook his head. He had no idea. No one had ever dared disobey Miss Hexx like that before.

12

How Miss Hexx longed for the days when you used to be able to hit disobedient children – with shoes and sticks and hands and bamboo canes and fishing rods and leather belts, to name just a few.

But she wasn't allowed to any more, so instead she had to content herself with telling Brandon how stupid he was, what a failure he was. He was a horrible selfish child who cared for no one except himself and no good would ever come of him.

'36,011,' said Brandon. '36,012, 36,013.'

'ARGGGH!' yelled Miss Hexx again.

She felt like strangling Brandon but that wasn't allowed either, so she turned around and strangled the curtains in her office instead.

Then she called Brandon's mum and told her she had to leave work right away and come and collect her child.

'I want that boy out of my school RIGHT NOW!' she roared.

'But he's only *counting*,' said Mum. 'It's educational.'

'Counting's only educational if you're counting something useful,' said Miss Hexx. 'Brandon isn't counting anything at all.'

'He's counting *numbers*,' said Mum.

'The numbers are already there. Nobody needs to count how many numbers there are.'

'But he's going up to TEN MILLION,' said Mum.

'So what? What's AT TEN MILLION?'

There was a pause.

'**36,163?**' said Brandon.

'Very funny. If he was counting apples, or money, or even stars, that might be useful. But numbers? I don't think so,' said Miss Hexx. 'Someone's already counted them or they wouldn't be there in the first place. If I were you, Mrs Wright, I'd take Brandon to the doctor. All this counting might be some kind of illness. I don't want the other children catching it.'

'But . . .'

'No buts. I *cannot* tolerate this sort of behaviour in my school. Take him away. And don't bring him back until this ridiculous counting has *stopped*.'

'Oh, Brandon,' said Mum, as they waited for the bus. 'They won't let you go to school and I can't leave you at home alone. But I need to work!

I don't know what to do.'

'37,557,' said Brandon sadly. He had no idea what she was going to do either. He only knew one thing. There were a lot of numbers between one and TEN MILLION, and every single one of them needed counting. He simply couldn't let them down.

'37,559,' he told his mother gently. And he smiled as number 37,559 did a somersault in the air for the sheer joy of having been counted so perfectly, before it melted into the air in a haze of grey and silver mist. Then number 37,600 swam towards Brandon with its arms wide open and a smile on its face as big as Christmas.

That afternoon, Mum tried everything she could to get Brandon to stop. She offered him treats, she offered him trips away. She offered games and prizes and toys. She offered him a new bike, which he'd wanted for ages.

When they didn't work, she tried to trick him.

'Would you like some biscuits, Brandon?' she said. 'How many?'

'44,011,' he said.

'Well, you can have three,' she said.

She tried singing counting songs to make him lose his place. She felt mean about it, but she was desperate. She tried shouting strange numbers in his ear. 'Two hundred, sixty-one thousand and twenty-ten,' she yelled. She tried blowing a trumpet at him and counting herself in the wrong direction.

None of it worked. Brandon just counted

the same as ever, undisturbed and perfect.

'Stop it, Mum,' shouted Elle in the end. 'Nothing can stop Brandon counting. Listen – it's so beautiful! Why don't you just *listen*?'

Mum sank on to the sofa and gave up. 'Yes, Elle,' she said. 'It is very, very beautiful. Beautiful – but useless. We can't eat it. It won't pay the rent or any of the bills, and . . .'

'45,161,' said Brandon softly. Mum bent her head and began to cry. Elle went to sit next to her to try and comfort her on one side, and Brandon came to sit on the other. He put his arm round her and gave her a big hug.

'45,165, 45,166,' he murmured lovingly.

He felt so sorry for her. He loved his mum so much, but he loved the numbers too. They had travelled from all over the universe to come and be counted by him.

What else could he do but count them? He had
no choice. He had to!

He had no space in his head for words to
say this, though. All he could do
was rub her cheek, feel the wet
of her tears on his hand
and murmur sweet
numbers to her.

'45,179,' he said.

Suddenly, Mum turned round to Brandon and took his face in her hands. She'd had enough.

'Brandon,' she said. 'It turns out that you're some kind of counting genius, but genius or not, it has to stop. It's stopping me working. If I don't go to work, we don't get any money. If we don't get any money, we can't pay the rent, and if we can't pay the rent we'll be thrown out and then we'll be homeless.'

Mum sighed. 'It's just our bad luck,' she said. 'You've found something you're really, really good at – and it's useless! So, Brandon – think about it, will you? I know what a sacrifice it must be – but please, Brandon. I'm asking you – I'm begging you, Brandon. Please stop counting!'

A couple of days later, Waris came round after school to film Brandon counting up to a hundred thousand. A crowd of children came with him. Mr Wyke came too and so did most of the other teachers at Todley Junior. Even teachers from other schools came – some because they just didn't believe it was possible for anyone to count so high and some because they wanted to see what a boy so naughty he wouldn't stop counting looked like.

But when they listened, all of them agreed that Brandon's counting was more beautiful than any counting they had ever heard before.

'I never even imagined that anyone could count so perfectly,' said one teacher. They all stayed as long as they could, just to listen. Brandon's mum had to kick everyone out in the end or they would have stayed all night.

That night, just before bedtime, Elle came to see Mum and told her Brandon had something to tell her. Mum's heart began to beat hard, because of course Brandon hadn't said anything except numbers for days now.

'Yes, Brandon?' she said, sitting down on the bed next to him. Brandon was tucked up, ready to sleep. He had his bear in bed next to him. Everything looked just the same as it had for the past three nights.

'107,269,' said Brandon.

There was a pause.

'Yes?' said Mum.

There was another pause.

'Brandon?' said Mum.

Brandon put his hands underneath his arms, closed his eyes tight and screwed up his face.

'Brandon! You've stopped, haven't you?'

Brandon bit his lip and nodded.

'Oh, Brandon!' said Mum. 'That's . . . that's such a big thing for you to do. I know how big it is. But . . . thank you, Brandon! Thank you so much! I know how important counting was to you. You've made life so much better for us all!'

She bent down to give him a big hug. Brandon hugged her back but he didn't say anything because he was trying so hard not to count. Number 107,270 was standing right there looking very upset!

But what could he do? Mums come first.

Elle began to cry with disappointment and Mum had to comfort her as well. Then she went to bed herself. She lay in the dark for a long time, unable to get to sleep. The house felt empty without the soft murmur of the numbers in the air. She felt sad at what she'd had to do. But no matter how long and hard she thought, she couldn't think of any way round it.

14

It was the middle of the night when Mum woke up again. She was sure she'd turned off all the lights when she went to bed and yet her room was bright with light.

She sat up. What a strange light it was! So clear and bright. It shimmered and shone in many different colours as if the air was made up of shining diamonds.

She got up and opened the door. The strange light was in the hall as well. Downstairs, she found Elle by the window on tiptoe, peering out of the glass. Mum looked over her shoulder into the night.

107,279, 107,280, 107,281, 107,282, 107,283, 107,284, 107,285, 107,286, 107,287, 107,288,

Cat

There was a stream
of that strange light,
twisting and turning
away from the house
up into the sky and
beyond to the stars.

'Numbers,'
whispered Mum.

107,289, 107,290, 107,291, 107,292, 107,293, 107,294, 107,295, 107,296, 107,297, 107,298, 107,299, 107,300

'They're still coming,' said Elle. 'Brandon might have stopped, but the numbers still want to be counted.'

Elle was right. Numbers, millions of them, were queueing up for their turn to be counted.

'They don't look very pleased,' said Mum.

'They're not,' said Elle, looking sharply at her.

Mum went upstairs to check on Brandon in his room, but the stairs were so thick with numbers it was like wading through water.

And it was bright! – The numbers shone like crystals. Upstairs, she had to shove and push to get Brandon's door open and when she finally got in, the room was shining so much she had to shield her eyes.

The numbers were up to some very funny tricks in there. Brandon's room was like a kaleidoscope. She could see everything eight times – his bed, his window, his chest of drawers, even the clothes and toys spread all over the floor. She went to him six or seven times to see if he was all right, but each time she got there it wasn't the real Brandon, it was a kaleidoscopic trick and she had to try again.

'Brandon! Are you all right? What's going on?' she asked when she finally found the real him.

Brandon didn't say anything, because if he opened his mouth the numbers would jump in to be counted. Instead he just smiled, spread his hands in the air and shrugged.

'This is ridiculous,' said Mum. She turned round to face the numbers.

'Out! Go on – out you go!' she shouted. **'All you numbers – out! Out, out, out!'**

She pushed and shoved and gradually, the numbers grumpily left the room, one after the other. It took her ten minutes to chase them all away. Some of them were hiding in the wardrobe and under the bed, and number 107,270 was clinging on to her back, so she never actually found that one at all.

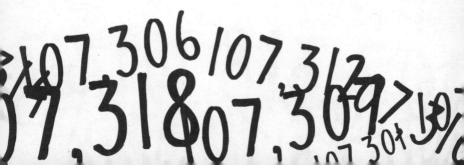

At last the room was clear. Mum fluffed up Brandon's covers and kissed him on the cheek.

'Night night, darling,' she murmured. 'You get a good night's sleep. They'll all be gone by the morning, I expect.'

Then she had to spend another ten or twenty minutes clearing all the numbers out of the rest of the house. When she was done, the place was normal again, but outside, the world looked like a gigantic kaleidoscope – eight moons, eight roads, eight everythings. And the moon and all the streetlamps were shining with all the colours of the spectrum. It was like being stuck inside a gigantic diamond. She was just taking Elle back to bed when she heard a funny noise from the window.

'What's that?' she said.

'It's the numbers,' said Elle. 'They're getting bored. I think they're going to undo the house.'

'Nonsense,' said Mum. 'Numbers can't do that. Can they?'

'Numbers,' said Elle, 'can do anything they want.'

There was a crack behind them. They turned to look. The numbers had taken the window neatly to pieces. The different pieces hung in the air a little apart from one another, as if they were about to be reassembled, like an exploded diagram.

There was a noise from the electrical sockets.

'There going to undo the plugs now,' said Elle.

'Don't be daft,' said Mum. But she didn't sound very convinced.

15

Later that morning, when Waris and Anandi came to take Elle to school, they saw the strangest thing. The whole house had been taken to bits in the night.

Each piece was floating in the air a few centimetres from where it should have been and the numbers were hovering above them showing their measurements. The roof was hovering above the house. The tiles were hovering above the roof. The bricks in the walls were all separated. Even the screws and nails had come out of the woodwork.

The whole house glowed in bright,

multicoloured   light
and there were numbers
everywhere – running across
the floors, circling the pots
and pans, measuring the stairs, doing
multiplication and long division
sums in the bathroom, working out the
bounce in the beds. It was a festival of numbers.
Waris borrowed his mum's phone
again to start filming it, but the numbers
started undoing that too. In a moment it
was hanging in bits and pieces in
the air, like everything else.

Mum and Elle were in the kitchen trying to get breakfast, which wasn't easy with everything floating around.

'Where's Brandon?' said Waris.

Mum pointed up.

Waris looked up. Sure enough, there was Brandon, with an enormous grin on his face, waving down from his bed, which was floating up in the air like a ship on an invisible sea.

Suddenly, the light went funny and split into colours.

'Here we go again,' sighed Brandon's mum. 'Watch yourselves!'

Everything went kaleidoscopic. There were eight of everything. Waris made a dash towards Brandon, but it was the wrong one and he banged his head on the door instead.

'Ouch!'

'Stay still,' warned Brandon's mum. 'You

just can't tell what's real and what's a number trick.' So they all stayed rooted to the spot for a few minutes, waiting for things to calm down.

'I wish they wouldn't do that,' said Mum. Her head had turned into a hexagon and she was trying to pour juice out of a jug shaped like an eternal spiral.

'This is ridiculous. You can't live like this!' cried Waris's mum.

'She's being very stubborn. She won't let Brandon start counting again,' said Elle, who was sitting at the table, which was floating in pieces above the tiles of the kitchen floor, trying to eat porridge. It was a messy business.

Anandi's chair began to come to pieces underneath her. '. . . But, Danielle, this is crazy!' she exclaimed. 'What are you going to *do*?'

'I'm not giving in,' insisted Mum. 'They'll get bored soon enough.'

'You wish,' muttered Elle.

Mum carried on trying to get breakfast ready, but it wasn't going well. She kept pouring milk into bowls and cups that were just reflections while the floorboards came to bits and got measured underneath her. Meanwhile, the windows and doors, the fridge and the washing machine, all became exploded diagrams.

Outside there was a loud *crump*! And a *bang*!

'Twelve cars have just crashed into twelve lampposts,' said Waris, looking out the window.

'Danielle,' said Waris's mum sternly, 'I'm sorry, but this has to stop. It's getting dangerous. Brandon is just going to have to start counting again, before these crazy numbers do something really silly.'

Mum paused. Above her, Brandon's head appeared over the edge of his bed with a hopeful expression on his face.

'You're going to have to let him sooner or later. It's only going to get worse,' said Elle.

'Oh – damn!' said Mum. 'I don't suppose there's any choice. OK, Brandon. Go on – get counting again. I'm sorry I stopped you. OK?'

A big, beautiful smile spread across Brandon's face. He sat up in bed, lifted up his arms, opened his mouth and said . . .

'107,270.'

All around the numbers stopped whatever it was they'd been up to and formed a queue – a long, long queue, that went all the way to the Milky Way. Ordered, waiting and ready. Number 107,270 went shimmering up to Heaven with a smile on its face and number 107,271 came cartwheeling towards him for its turn.

All the things that had been undone started to come together again – the house, the car, the streetlamps outside. Brandon's bed got lower and lower to the ground and landed neatly just as the last screw in the window went back home, where it had all started the night before.

'107,271,' said Brandon happily. '107,272, 107,273.' All around him, TEN MILLION numbers breathed a big sigh of relief. Numbers 107,271, 107,272 and 107,273 spun up into the air with pure happiness, and number 107,274 came shyly forward to take its turn to be named.

Waris ran over to pick up his mum's phone which lay on the floor all in one piece again. He gave it a big kiss.

107,272

107,273

107,271

'Thank Heaven you're safe, my darling,' he said. The screen lit up. Waris peered anxiously at it. 'It's our YouTube channel,' he said. 'And . . . look!'

He held up the phone for everyone to see. On the screen was an image of Brandon counting to one hundred thousand. Underneath that was another number. And that number kept going up.

'Five hundred thousand,' said Waris. 'No – 501,200. No – 504,700! Wow!'

It was the number of Brandon's views. Overnight, Dame Mildred Gosling, the world's most famous mathematician, had spotted Brandon counting to one hundred thousand and she'd tweeted about it.

The most perfect counting I've ever heard, she'd tweeted.

Now everyone wanted to see it. Brandon's views were going up by the second.

'Over five hundred thousand views already,' shouted Waris. 'I was right. Brandon is AMAZING!'

'I'll have a look at that, thank you,' said a voice.

A hand reached down over Waris's shoulder and snatched the phone out of his hand.

'Hey,' said Waris.

It was Miss Hexx. She'd let herself into the house without knocking.

'505,968 views, quite right,' said Miss Hexx. 'Marvellous. What a good job I turned up. This situation is going to need managing.'

'I'm Brandon's manager,' said Waris.

Miss Hexx didn't answer. She was staring at Brandon as if he were made out of pure money.

'Brandon Wright, you have a gift – and if we play this right we're all going to be stinking rich,' she said. 'I want a new school. A bigger school. A more *important* school. And you, Brandon Wright . . . you're going to help me get it!'

Straight away she sat down with Mum, pulled out her laptop and started typing up a contract then and there. In the middle of it all, Brandon sat on the sofa, counting quietly away.

'Oh, Brandon,' said Elle. 'You've gone and done it now, haven't you?'

Brandon sighed. '108,345,' he said. '108,346, 108,347.'

16

Brandon was an overnight counting sensation.

All over the world, people were going on YouTube to watch him count. The views went up and up and up. Later that day, Dame Mildred Gosling herself put in a call.

'Brandon,' she said. 'I'm an old, old lady, and like you I've loved numbers all my life. If I have just one wish before I die, it would be to listen in while you count up to my favourite number – **186,282**, the speed of light. I would give anything to be allowed to do that.'

'118,029,' said Brandon.

'Thank you,' said Dame Mildred.

Dame Mildred had to fly back from Moscow, where she was giving a lecture on the mathematics of black holes, but she was round at Brandon's door at half-past eight a couple of days later, to hear him count. Miss Hexx had organised all the news channels and papers to be there so the meeting with the old lady who loved numbers and the young boy whom the numbers loved could be viewed by the whole nation.

Dame Mildred shook Brandon by the hand and said it was a pleasure to meet him. She called him a National Treasure.

'184,401,' said Brandon.

Dame Mildred nodded. 'I understand,' she said.

They sat in the sitting room while Brandon counted. When he reached 186,282, she burst into tears.

'It was the most wonderful experience of my life,' she sobbed. 'It was like being a girl again, discovering the beauty of numbers for the first time. Thank you, Brandon. Thank you so much.'

That night, the world watched on YouTube as the world's most famous mathematician wept for joy at hearing her favourite number counted. Brandon's views went up faster than ever.

Before she left, Mum had a quiet word with Dame Mildred. She told her about how the numbers had taken the house to bits when Brandon stopped counting.

'You must be very careful not to stop him again,' Dame Mildred told her. 'Numbers can be very useful, but they can also be very secretive and wicked too if they want. This time it was your house. Next time it could be worse. They could take the country to pieces if they wanted. They could make the stock market crash, or make the moon fall down. They could even stop the sun shining if they felt like it.

'Take my advice, Mrs Wright – just let him count.'

By the next morning, Brandon had over ten million views on YouTube.

#brandonweloveyou

#countinggenius

#theresnoonelikebrandon

#thebigonemillion

Four weeks later, Brandon reached his first million. Miss Hexx had arranged for a public count. It was going to be the biggest event the little town of Todley had ever seen.

People arrived by the coachload. There were extra trains carrying extra passengers. There was a funfair and a market and the shops were open all hours. There were jugglers, musicians and performing mathematicians lining the streets. Everyone was busy buying Brandon flags and Big Count badges before going into the school grounds, where they passed under a big flashing neon sign:

THE BIG ONE MILLION

Then they followed a trail of number flags towards the Big Count Marquee where Brandon was going to perform the first one million in counting history.

Tickets were twenty pounds each and every last one had been sold. In fact, there were so many people wanting to watch, they couldn't all fit in the marquee so the mayor had put a Big Count Big Screen up outside the Town Hall so that even those who couldn't get in could watch it live.

Brandon was in his dressing room counting away with Elle and Waris by his side. Miss Hexx was running around behind the scenes with a cameraman and an assistant cameraman, making sure she got Brandon from all angles as he built up to the Big One Million for a film she was going to make.

'Brandon – move those lips!' she commanded. 'People don't just want to hear the BIG ONE MILLION – they want to see it too!'

'999,567, 999,568,' said Brandon, flapping his lips as much as he could.

'Cameras roll!' yelled Miss Hexx.

Outside they could hear the murmur of the crowds as they took their seats. There were thousands of people out there.

'Aren't you nervous, Brandon?' asked Elle, who was sitting next to him holding his hand tightly. She had noticed he was trembling.

'999,633th,' said Brandon. The 'th' came because the make-up woman accidentally got her powder puff in his mouth as she was dusting his face.

'Careful!' said Elle.

'It has to be done, he ought to stay quiet while I'm working on him,' said the make-up woman.

'He can't. He's counting,' said Waris. He rolled his eyes at Brandon. He was feeling fed up because even though he had made Brandon a star on YouTube, Miss Hexx had banned him from taking any unauthorised pictures. Instead, he had to interview Brandon for the school magazine. He sighed and picked up his pen and notepad.

'So, Brandon,' he said. 'How does it feel to be the world's greatest counting sensation?

Brandon rolled his eyes. '999,651, 999,652,' he said.

★

Miss Hexx had finished filming Brandon and now she was outside on stage making a speech to the crowd about the Big Count Schools she was going to build with all the money they were making.

'It's easy to tell what a marvellous headteacher I am,' she bellowed. 'Because it was from *my* school that the counting marvel that is Brandon Wright came. I helped and encouraged him. I developed and nurtured his love of numbers. It's all about me!'

Mum came bustling in to the dressing room.

'OK, Brandon. OK, Elle,' she said. 'Are you ready?'

'OK,' said Elle.

'999,853,' said Brandon.

Mum looked into Brandon's very white face, and kneeled down by his side.

'Brandon,' she said. 'I want you to know how proud I am of you. I know that all this must be difficult sometimes . . .'

'999,859,' agreed Brandon.

'. . . but we are making a lot of money out of it. We'll be able to buy a new house of our own soon, and I can put some money away for you and Elle. A chance like this comes along once in a lifetime. We have to make the most of it. You do understand, don't you?'

'999,863,' said Brandon, nodding. Yes, he understood. He just wished . . . he just wished there weren't so many people out there.

'OK.' Mum stood up. 'Let's go.'

The crowd went crazy when they saw Brandon coming onto the stage.

'Bran-don! Bran-don! Bran-don!' they shouted.

'Listen to me, everyone,' shouted Miss Hexx. 'We are about to witness a very special event. A record-breaking event. One lonely but very special child – a pupil at my school – will reach a number unheard of in the annals of counting. What is that child's name?'

'BRANDON!'

roared ten thousand voices.

'And what is that number?' she yelled.

'ONE MILLION!' yelled the crowd.

'And who's going to do it with him?' yelled Miss Hexx.

'WE ARE!' yelled the crowd.

Everything went very quiet as Brandon counted up towards one million. At 999,990 Miss Hexx gave the signal for the crowd to count up with him. She was getting more and more excited as they got close.

'GO GO GO!' she yelled.

'999,997,' said Brandon.

'WE'RE SOOOOOO CLOSE!' bellowed Miss Hexx.

'999,998,' said Brandon.

'WAIT FOR IT, WAIT FOR IT!' roared Miss Hexx.

'999,999 . . .'

'OH MY GOD HERE IT COMES!'

'ONE MILLION!'

screamed the crowd, all together. Brandon stood up
and punched the air above his head.

'BRAN-DON BRAN-DON BRAN-DON!'

shouted the crowd. Mum wept with pride. Waris jumped up and down screamed with excitement. Everyone cheered and cheered until their throats were sore.

Brandon sat quietly down. '1,000,001,' he said. '1,000,002, 1,000,003.'

'My brother,' said Elle. 'He's unbelievable!'

It was all a huge success. Everyone made lots of money out of it. The only people who weren't happy were the mathematicians.

'It was very exciting,' said Dame Mildred on TV that evening. 'The only problem was, with so many people counting with him, the simple, perfect beauty of Brandon's counting got drowned out.'

'Ridiculous,' said Miss Hexx. 'Anyone can count. It isn't the counting itself that's special – it's how it's *presented*.'

#thebigtwomillion

#brandonisthegreatest

#countingsuperstarbrandonwright

At the BIG TWO MILLION, ticket prices had gone up to fifty pounds. There was no marquee in the world big enough to hold all the people who wanted to see it, so it was held in the open air on the school playing fields.

Brandon, Elle and Mum had moved out of their damp little house by the canal and moved up the hill to a big house with a garden, a trampoline and an indoor swimming pool.

It was very nice, except that Miss Hexx kept coming round to film them, or to show them off to people who wanted to put some money into the Big Count School, so they never got much time to just enjoy it.

Sometimes Big Count fans would sneak in through the gates or over the fence to get Brandon's autograph. Two of them even managed to corner him when he was in the toilet and wouldn't let him pull up his pants until he'd signed their workbooks.

He and Elle didn't go to school any more because so many fans kept turning up trying to catch a glimpse of Brandon. Instead, Mr Wyke came round every day to home tutor them. They liked Mr Wyke, but both of them missed their friends at school. Waris visited from time to time, but not often. Miss Hexx had caught him trying to sneak out some photos of Brandon counting at home, and after that she wouldn't let him come round unsupervised.

'Anyway, he's not clever enough for you,' she told Brandon. 'Only the best for my little gold mine.'

Sometimes, even though Brandon had millions of fans all over the world, he felt very lonely.

The BIG TWO MILLION was big but the BIG THREE MILLION was even bigger! It was going to be bigger than the other two millions put together. Miss Hexx had knocked down the school to make way for the Big Count Stadium, seating over fifty thousand people. Tickets cost one hundred pounds each and big screens had been set up in towns and villages all over the North West, so everyone could see local superstar Brandon Wright.

It was a pity about the old school. Brandon and the other children had all been fond of it. But Miss Hexx had built a new school that was bigger and much better than the old one – The Big Count School for Talented Children. Not all the children from the old school went to it, because you had to pass a special exam to get in.

'A successful school only has room for successful children,' said Miss Hexx. So many of Brandon's old friends had to get re-schooled elsewhere. Not that Brandon had much time for them anyway. He was far too busy counting at special executive dinners, festivals, football matches, rock stars' parties and other special events to have time for anything ordinary like that.

'I'm just a bit worried that he should be spending more time with his friends and being a normal child,' Mum said to Miss Hexx.

'Nonsense! Brandon is ANYTHING but normal,' said Miss Hexx. 'Anyway, you signed a contract.'

It was true. Mum re-read the contract and it did say that Brandon had to do whatever his manager needed him to do to improve his brand. And his manager was . . . Miss Hexx.

The BIG FOUR MILLION was going to be bigger than the other three millions put together.

Tickets cost two hundred pounds each and Fat Plum Computers were paying Hexx's Big Count Schools PLC an extra six-figure sum for Brandon's first words after he got to ten million. They wanted him to say, 'I'd never have done it without a Fat Plum laptop.'

The money was due on the day he arrived at the BIG TEN MILLION.

'What if he doesn't get there?' asked Mum.

'He better had,' said Miss Hexx. 'It says so in the contract you signed.'

The BIG FIVE MILLION was going to be

ENORMOUS

– bigger than the other four millions put together. Ticket prices had gone up to three hundred pounds each and cinemas and football stadiums all over the country were showing it live. A boy in China, a girl in the USA and a pair of twins in Russia had started rival counts of their own.

Miss Hexx found out that Mr Wyke had spoken to a reporter on one of the Sunday papers without her permission, about teaching Brandon at home so she decided that he wasn't a good enough teacher for Brandon.

'But we like him,' said Mum.

'I don't care if you like him or not, he's not good enough,' said Miss Hexx.

'Brandon's my son and I'll be the one who decides who teaches him,' said Mum.

'No, you won't,' said Miss Hexx. 'Read the contract.'

So she did. Miss Hexx was right again.

19

At the **BIG SIX MILLION** the Minister for Education came to give a speech about the value of counting. Miss Hexx was given a medal for services to education, and Mum bought a field behind the new house to keep horses in.

Brandon had his own personal trainer to make sure he was fit and healthy for the Big Count. He was so busy flying all over the country doing public counts, he barely ever saw his mum, or Elle or Waris.

'He needs time to play,' said Mum.

'He can't have it,' said Miss Hexx. 'Read the contract.'

It was true. The contract said Brandon didn't have any time for play at all.

The **BIG SEVEN MILLION** was going to be

VAST

– bigger than the other six millions all put together.

Ticket prices had gone up to five hundred pounds each and cinemas all over the world were showing it live. A Hollywood film company bought the rights to make a film called *The Ten Million Kid* and a West End theatre bought the rights to the musical. They both offered a fortune. The money was due the day after the **BIG TEN MILLION** was done.

The girl from the USA had a nervous breakdown and was not allowed to count any more. The boy in China was found to be using a computer to help him, so he was disqualified. The twins from Russia were counting so fast, they were catching up quick, but they were still 2,400,017 behind Brandon.

Brandon was given a personal doctor and a personal mathematician to go with his personal massage therapist.

A Chinese billionaire had offered a million pounds for a five-minute private chat with Brandon. Miss Hexx spent three days trying to convince Brandon to stop counting for just five minutes to talk. But Brandon didn't answer. Miss Hexx tore at her hair in a fury.

'ALL HE EVER DOES IS COUNT!'

she shrieked.

'This is *your* fault,' she told Mum. 'It's your job to make him speak to Mr Wu!'

'Well, I won't,' said Mum. 'My Brandon's a counter, not a talker.'

'We'll see about that,' said Miss Hexx.

The BIG EIGHT MILLION was going to be

GIGANTIC

– more ENORMOUS and VASTER and HUGER than all the other seven millions put together.

The twins from Russia got shut down because they were taking it in turns, so although it looked as though they were up to 7,500,000, they'd really only counted half of that each.

Brandon was given a personal tutor and a personal playmate to go with his personal trainer and his personal physician.

'He doesn't need a personal playmate. He can play with Waris. Waris is his friend,' said Mum.

'Waris isn't in the contract as a playmate,' said Miss Hexx.

'Or Elle . . .' said Mum.

'Neither is she,' said Miss Hexx. 'And actually, neither are you either, so don't ask.'

20

It was the day of the **BIG NINE MILLION**. Brandon was in his dressing room high above the stands of the Big Count Stadium, looking out of his window at the thousands of people who had paid eight hundred pounds each to hear him count up to nine million.

The **BIG NINE MILLION** – well, you get the picture. It was going to be

GINORMOUS!

So many people! Even through the triple glazing of his dressing-room suite, he could hear the roar of thousands of voices.

'BRAN-DON BRAN-DON BRAN-DON!'

they roared.

'8,999,819,' trembled Brandon.

He'd never been so scared in all his life.

So many people!

. . . So many numbers . . .

So much going on!

'I think he's going to be sick,' whispered Elle to Mum. 'He looks really ill.'

But Brandon was surrounded by so many people, Mum couldn't get near him. His personal trainer was shouting – 'One, two! One, two! One, two!' as Brandon did his jogging on the spot. His personal massage therapist was rubbing his back for him. His personal doctor was dosing him with anti-sickness serum and vitamins. His personal coach was counting up the numbers with him, his personal mathematician was checking that the numbers were in the right

order for counting before they were allowed
anywhere near him and his personal playmate
was letting him win at *Kill All Enemies*.

'BRANDON!' shouted Mum, over the
heads of all those people. 'ARE YOU OK?'

'I think he's scared, Mum,' said Elle.

'8,999,867 . . .' murmured Brandon faintly.

'You don't have to do
it if you don't want to,'
said Mum.

'What? Of COURSE he has to do it!' screeched Miss Hexx, swooping down on her in her expensive new designer suit. 'Do you have any idea how much money we'd lose if he doesn't do it? Why do you think we have all these people here . . .?'

'One, two! One, two! One, two!' shouted the personal trainer.

'Six to you, only two to me,' said his personal playmate.

'Snack time,' said his personal nutritionist. 'Spaghetti hoops three ways, you ate two, four, six, ten, sixteen . . .'

The people swam before Brandon's eyes.

So did the numbers.

'Look at us, Brandon!' they called. 'Count us, count us.'

'BRAN-DON BRAN-DON!' yelled the crowd.

'BRANDON!' yelled Mum.

'HE MUST COUNT! He must count! He must count, count, count, count, count!' screeched Miss Hexx.

Suddenly, it was all too much. Brandon was sick all down his orange Big Count uniform . . . and fainted.

It was awful. The Big Count Nine Million had to be delayed for over an hour while Brandon was sorted out. The numbers got bored and started undoing the Big Count Stadium, which cost tens of thousands of pounds to repair. The TV stations had to pay money to their advertisers for not having the BIG NINE MILLION at the right time.

It was a disaster. Miss Hexx knew exactly who to blame for it.

'You put him off by shouting at him,' she told Mum.

'I was only trying to see if he was all right,' said Mum. 'I couldn't get near him for all those people.'

'Those people were professionals trying to make sure Brandon did his job properly,' said Miss Hexx. 'What's more, as the mother, it was

YOUR job to make sure Brandon got onto the stage on time, and you failed to do it. So I'm sorry to say this, Mrs Wright – but you're fired!'

'You can't sack me, I'm his mother!' shouted Mum.

'It's in the contract. I think you'll find I can.'

Miss Hexx took Mum to court for abuse of a minor and breach of contract. Mum lost and Brandon was taken out of her care and put under the guardianship of Miss Hexx.

He was only allowed to see his family once a fortnight under strict supervision.

'What about me?' asked Waris.

'You're sacked too,' said Miss Hexx.

21

#thebigtenmillion

#brandonsuperstar

#ilovebrandon

#alliwantforchristmasisbrandon

#butcanhereallydoit

#ANDWHATWILLHEDONEXT

#ANDWHATWILLHESAY

The BIG TEN MILLION.

It was going to be simply

ENORMOUS!!

Miss Hexx had lost a fortune on the BIG NINE MILLION and she was determined to make it all back and much, much more at the BIG TEN MILLION.

Of course there was a lot of money to be made at the count itself, but there was still more money to be made afterwards. What would Brandon's first words be when he finally got to TEN MILLION? Why had he counted so high? What would he do next?

These were the questions the world wanted to know. And big companies were prepared to pay a lot of money for those first words. The contract with Fat Plum Computers had been signed and a host of other big companies were lining up to buy the second, third, fourth, fifth and sixth things he said, right the way up to several hundred.

Playtendo wanted him to make an advert and say, 'At last I can have a go on my Playtendo Big Box.' They were offering an eight-figure sum, too.

The businessman had now offered twenty million pounds to speak to him in private as soon as he'd finished. He wanted to keep Brandon's words of wisdom all to himself. Miss Hexx had been very tempted, but the Prime Minister herself had been in touch and asked her not to.

'Brandon belongs to the nation,' she said. 'Every child deserves the right to be inspired by Brandon.'

'They do if they pay for it,' said Miss Hexx. But she agreed anyway, in exchange for a big tax break for Hexx's Big Count Schools PLC.

At last the big day came.

The **BIG TEN MILLION**.

It had taken Brandon nearly a year to get there. When he started out, no one even knew who he was. Now, he was world famous and one of the richest boys on earth. But he had lost his friends – he hadn't seen Waris for weeks. He'd lost his family – he'd only been allowed to see them once a fortnight since Miss Hexx sacked Mum. His old school had been knocked down. He hadn't eaten a meal in peace or played on his own for months. If it hadn't been for the numbers, he'd have been the loneliest boy in the world.

Miss Hexx had decided that there had been too many people around for the **BIG NINE MILLION**, so she was making sure that things were kept very quiet this time. Brandon had been fed on a balanced diet of nutritious brain food. Fish, mainly. Only one person was allowed to be in the same room as him at a time. He had been banned from seeing his family altogether – he got too upset whenever Miss Hexx explained to him why they were a bad influence, so it was best for him not to see them at all.

How Brandon was looking forward to it all being over and done, so he could get back to being normal! Playing games with his friends, being kissed goodnight by his mum, eating pizza and boasting about things he had no chance of ever really doing. The good old days. How he longed to go back to them! But he knew in his heart that those days were still a long way off . . .

The Big Count itself was being held in Wembley Stadium – the only stadium in the country big enough to hold all the people who wanted to watch it at one thousand pounds a ticket. Brandon was in his dressing room, high up above the stage, all alone except for his personal quiet coach, who was playing soothing music on his lute and checking that the scent wafters he'd installed were putting out the right kind of gentle, soothing odours.

No disturbing, upsetting sounds from outside could get into his sound-proofed booth. The windows had all been blacked out so he couldn't see the ninety thousand people who had come to hear him count to **TEN MILLION.**

'9,999,872, 9,999,873,' said Brandon.

Very quietly at the back of the padded room, a door opened. Brandon's quiet coach slipped out and in came Miss Hexx.

'Brandon,' she whispered. She kneeled

'9,999,883,' said Brandon.

down by his side and held his hand.

'I've done a fantastic job for you, Brandon,' whispered Miss Hexx. 'The **BIG TEN MILLION** is everywhere. On social media. TV. Radio. In the newspapers and magazines.

'Every town centre in the WORLD has a big screen up so that people can see. Cinemas are showing it. Football games have been cancelled so that people can go into the stadia and watch

125

it there.

'Millions of people all over the world are relying on you, Brandon. Can you imagine how disappointed they'll be if you let them down, like last time?' She shook her head sadly. 'No one will like you or love you. You'd break your fans' poor hearts. Your friends will desert you. Even your mother and your sister – remember, them, Brandon? – even they would never want to see you again.

'Wouldn't that be *terrible*, Brandon? Don't you think?'

Brandon nodded sadly.

'OK,' whispered Miss Hexx. 'Then let's go.'

22

Brandon was going to perform the **BIG TEN MILLION** inside a glass ball on top of a tall tower in the middle of Wembley Stadium where everyone could get a clear view of him. It was so high, he had to be taken up in a lift.

All up and down the tower there were giant screens showing adverts and favourite Big Count moments from past months. The stadium was surrounded by cranes with cameras on them. Drones hovered around him, taking shots from unusual angles. All around, there were big screens up so that people could see every twitch of his lips and hear every breath he took.

From up there on high, you could see the whole stadium and beyond, far over London. It was a beautiful day. The sun shone, brightening up the towers of the city. Down at Brandon's feet, in the stadium and the streets beyond, hundreds of thousands of people had gathered to hear him. Brandon peered down and tried to see if his mum and Elle were there, but he was too high up and couldn't make out if they were.

9,999,891, 9,999,892, 9,999,893, 9,999,894, 9,999,895, 9,999,896, 9,999,897, 9,999,898, 9,999,899,

He sighed and lifted his eyes to the sky. There were an awful lot of numbers up there. Brandon didn't think Miss Hexx was going to be very happy with him when she found out just how many . . .

A famous celebrity presenter was up there with Brandon and Miss Hexx in the glass bubble. This was the biggest event he had ever done and he was feeling very nervous about the whole thing.

'A big, Big Count welcome to our viewers all over the world. It's THE BIG TEN MILLION!' he said.

All over the world, people cheered and leaned in closer to their TV sets.

'A big hello from me. And a big hello from Miss Big Count herself – Headteacher of Hexx's Big Count Schools PLC, Delia Hexx!'

Miss Hexx jumped to her feet. 'None of this would ever have happened if it weren't for me and my school!' she yelled. 'Remember to donate to Big Count Schools and to buy Big Count raffle tickets, and maybe your child can be lucky enough to go to one!'

'Thank you, Delia. And now here's the star of the show – Brandon Wright himself! So, Brandon. This is it! What you've been working for all these months. Are you ready for the big day?' asked the presenter. All over the world, millions of viewers and listeners leaned forward in case Brandon spoke.

'9,999,973,' said Brandon, nodding his head.

'Brilliant,' said the presenter.

'Nothing can stop Brandon,' said Miss Hexx.

'Miss Hexx,' the presenter said. 'The Big Count is being broadcast all over the world. People everywhere are waiting to hear what

Brandon is going to say next. Does anyone have any *idea* what that's going to be?'

'No one knows,' said Miss Hexx mysteriously. 'It's one of the world's biggest and most wonderful secrets.'

Brandon was up to 9,999,988.

'OK,' said the presenter. 'It's time for the **BIG COUNTDOWN!** All together with Brandon . . .'

'9,999,990,' said Brandon calmly.

'9,999,991!' screamed the world. The glass bubble on top of the tower quivered as if it had been struck.

'If they shout any louder we'll shatter,' muttered the presenter anxiously.

'9,999,992,' said Brandon, and the world shouted it with him.

'9,999,993!'

Up he counted,

up and up to the highest number anyone had ever counted to.

Up, up, up . . .

'9,999,997,' said Brandon.

'GET READY FOR THE BIG TEN MILLION!' shouted Miss Hexx.

'9,999,998,' said Brandon.

'GO BRANDON GO GO GO GO GO!' screamed Miss Hexx.

'9,999,999.'

'Now, Brandon NOW! GIVE IT TO US!'

'EVERYONE BE QUIET!'

shouted the presenter. 'We all want to hear it. Brandon?'

Brandon paused for a moment . . .

. . . just long enough for the whole world to hold its breath . . .

. . . just long enough for the world to go as still as it could . . .

. . . just long enough to make the right amount of space and quietness needed for what he needed to do . . .

And then he waited a little longer . . .

'Brandon!' hissed Miss Hexx.

'Go on!' hissed the presenter.

. . . and Brandon waited just one second longer, so everyone in the whole world was holding their breaths . . .

And then he said: '9,999,998.'

'What?' said the presenter.

'What?' exclaimed Miss Hexx.

'9,999,997,' said Brandon. '9,999,996.'

'He's started to count back down to nothing!' yelled the presenter.

'NO!' screamed Miss Hex. She jumped and grabbed Brandon by the throat. At the same time, the presenter jumped up and grabbed his neck from the back.

'Say it! Say it! The BIG TEN MILLION!' they both yelled. But Miss Hexx and the presenter had forgotten for a moment that the whole world was watching them. Suddenly, they heard a nasty hissing sound behind them. They turned, their hands still wrapped around Brandon's neck.

'9,999,991,' gurgled Brandon.

What they saw far below were not the bright happy faces of a moment ago. Instead, they saw hordes of ugly, angry faces. Disappointed faces. The faces of people who felt they had been cheated.

'CHEAT, CHEAT, CHEAT!' they were yelling. And even worse – 'WE WANT OUR MONEY BACK!' People were waving their fists at them. Some of them were trying to charge the tower with the glass bubble on top.

'Let's get out of here,' said Miss Hexx.

They all jumped in the lift and headed down, down, down to the ground. Even in the lift they could hear the crowd banging on the door below and shouting abuse.

'Cheat! Liars! Frauds!'

'We want our ten million!' they shouted.

'We're ruined!' wailed Miss Hexx. 'No one's going to pay you for counting down to nothing! Brandon – I'm going to sue you for this . . .'

'9,999,990,'

said Brandon.

'Shut up!' screamed Miss Hexx, right in his face.

The door to the tower lift opened – and there was an angry crowd of people all thirsting for revenge.

'HERE HE IS!' shouted Miss Hexx. 'THIS IS THE BOY WHO LET YOU ALL DOWN. THIS IS THE LIAR. HE'S THE ONE YOU WANT – CHEATING BRANDON WRIGHT!'

The crowd screamed in rage, but before they could get him, an arm shot out of the crowd and grabbed him by the collar.

It was Mum.

'This way, Brandon!' she shouted. She tugged him away from Miss Hexx's clutching fingers and pushed him through the crowd. In front of them was Mr Wyke and a group of determined mathematicians, shoving and pushing the crowd back.

'GET THEM!' yelled Miss Hexx.

The crowd turned to follow, but Mum was fast and those mathematicians were tough as boulders. She pushed and pulled Brandon past the grasping hands and clutching fingers, sliding and turning and dodging and twisting until they were lost in the crowd. They ran towards the tunnel.

'9,999,967,' panted Brandon. '9,999,966.'

In the tunnel, Elle and Dame Mildred Gosling were waiting in a fast car. They bundled Brandon in the back of it, and drove off as quickly as they could, out of the stadium, out of Wembley, out of London – and away up the motorway to their own homes in the lovely North.

'One thing puzzles me, Brandon,' said Dame Mildred as they sped up the M6. 'Why did you stop at 9,999,999 and start going down again? I mean, what happened to ten million?'

'9,999,907,' said Brandon.

'Perhaps number ten million was busy doing something else,' suggested Elle.

Dame Mildred thought about it. 'I see,' she said. 'But why start counting back down, then? It's the same numbers, after all.'

'9,999,901,' said Brandon.

'No,' said Elle. 'The numbers going down are different from the ones going up. They just have the same names, that's all.'

'Really? Different from the ones going up? I never knew that. Fascinating,' said Dame Mildred. And she took out her notebook and started trying to work out why.

'9,999,889,' said Brandon happily. He was back with his family. From now on, he was sure, everything was going to be all right.

23

#Brandoncheat

#Brandonwehateyou

#BigBigLoser

#everybodyhatesbrandonwright

#GETBRANDONWRIGHT

T he newspaper headlines the next day said:

A NATION'S SHAME.

There was a big picture of Brandon underneath it.

And . . .

YOU LET US DOWN, BRANDON.

And . . .

BRANDON – GO BACK TO SCHOOL AND SHUT UP

And . . .

CHEAT!

Miss Hexx had bet everything on the BIG TEN MILLION. Not only that, she had bet all of Brandon and Mum's money on it as well.

They lost their big mansion and their posh car and had to move back into their old, cold little house. Everyone who loved Brandon yesterday hated him today. Each day the postman would bring bags full of hate mail from their enemies. People threw rotten eggs and stones at the windows and pushed paper bags with dog poo through the letterbox.

People shouted at them in the street. The shops refused to serve them. Brandon and Elle went back to school and got bullied. Mum tried to get her old job back but the boss said that she wasn't the sort of person he wanted working for any company of his.

'Ten million indeed. What a con,' he said. 'My sister paid a fortune for a seat to watch that.'

Things got so bad, they had to move to another part of town. Brandon and Elle went to a new school, but their faces were so well known they got bullied there, too. Even the teachers made sarcastic remarks like, 'I suppose there's not much point in me teaching you anything, Brandon Wright, because you know it already, I expect.'

And all the time, Brandon was counting down . . .

8,799,663, 8,799,662, 8,799,661, . . .

The family did have some friends. Waris came to visit when he could and played computer games.

'It was fun while it lasted, Brandon,' he said. 'But you see, I knew you were just boasting. Of course, no one could ever really count up to ten million.'

'8,513,017,' said Brandon.

'You fooled everyone else but you couldn't fool me. Fancy a game?'

The bullying at school got so bad that Brandon and Elle got expelled for being troublemakers. Fortunately, Mr Wyke and some of the mathematicians agreed to come and teach them at home during the day, while Mum was out trying to find a job. That helped. Whenever she left the house, she had to disguise herself as a man, with a false beard and baggy trousers and speak in a gruff voice.

Dame Mildred Gosling came round to see them from time to time. The numbers sounded just as lovely to her as they always had. She was trying to develop a new theory about the numbers going up and the numbers going down. It was going to be called The Gosling-Wright Theory of Directional Counting.

She always gave the family some money to live off, if she had any spare. Sometimes she brought round other mathematician friends to listen to the numbers as well, and they always paid for the pleasure. If it wasn't for them, Brandon and his family would have gone very hungry indeed.

It was half-term and Brandon was still counting down. 8,301,703, 8,301,702, 8,301,701, 8,301,700.

Miss Hexx's chain of Big Count Schools for Talented Children had been taken away from her and put into special measures, and she had been banned from education for life.

She soon bounced back though, when she started selling her story to the newspapers for a lot of money.

THE DAILY SUN

'I was Ruined by Cheating Brandon'

WEATHER IN YOUR AREA

COMPETITION!
★WIN★

◀ MAIL DAY ▶

How Brandon Wright was ruined by his own lying family

THE SUNDAY PAPER
'Brandon Wright likes drowning kittens in his spare time!'

None of this was true, but everyone believed it anyway. Brandon and his family got more hate mail and abuse in the streets than ever. Everyone felt sorry for Miss Hexx.

Brandon was still counting down . . .

'7,277,709, 7,277,708, 7,277,707.'

Mum managed to get a little job at a bread factory, carrying heavy bags of flour for the bakers. She had to put her hair and her fake beard in a hairnet and came back at the end of each day exhausted and covered in flour.

Mr Wyke came round, once a week. Sometimes he bought Mum flowers and chocolates and wanted her to go out with him to the cinema. She did from time to time, but she was so tired she always fell asleep in her seat and he had to wake her up when the film ended and tell her what had happened.

Brandon and Elle got pretty lonely as well but at least they had each other – and the numbers. Some of them had grown so fond of Brandon that they stayed on and did tricks for them in their bedrooms.

◎

Autumn turned to winter. Brandon was still counting down. '6,068,971, 6,068,970, 6,068,969,'

Someone discovered where the family was living and so they had to move house again because the hate mail and the abuse started up once more. Mum lost her job when she got too close to the ovens and the glue that kept her beard on melted.

Christmas came. They had no money at all and it was the most miserable Christmas morning ever. Just like Miss Hexx had said, they had cold baked beans for Christmas dinner and they had to make presents for each other out of old newspapers.

But then, that afternoon, there was a knock at the door. At first Mum wouldn't answer it in case it was another delivery of dog poo. But it was Dame Mildred with Mr Wyke and some mathematician friends.

'SURPRISE!' They all shouted. And . . .

'Happy Christmas!'

They had brought a big Christmas hamper, lots of presents wrapped up in brightly coloured paper, some bottles of champagne and juice, decorations, nuts, a fruit basket, sugared figs, plums and tiny little oranges wrapped in paper, a new smart TV and an entire roast turkey, still hot, all wrapped up in silver foil.

151

Mum wept. Mr Wyke gave her a bunch of flowers and asked her out on another date. Then they had a proper Christmas dinner with crackers and paper hats and rubbish jokes.

Later in the evening, Brandon and Elle got the numbers to do some tricks on the floor of the living room while everyone watched in amazement. Suddenly, Dame Mildred jumped to her feet.

'Wait a minute!' she shouted. 'That's the Riemann hypothesis. You've just proved the Riemann hypothesis! How did you do that?'

'**5,665,327**,' said Brandon.

'We didn't do anything,' said Elle. 'The numbers did it.'

And then . . .

'Hang on!' shouted someone else. 'Is that minus zero? What are you doing with minus zero, Brandon? You can't do that – it doesn't even exist!'

'That one just came for a visit,' said Elle.

Suddenly everything got very noisy as the

mathematicians started spotting tricks the numbers were doing. The room was full of cries of . . .

'Look! P versus NP! How did they do that?'

'Is that the Hodge conjecture behind the sofa?'

'Oh my Lord, look! There's the Yang-Mills existence and mass gap problem being solved on the mantelpiece!'

Finally one mathematician saw a unified field theory going up the chimney and tried to chase after it and got stuck. It took them half an hour to get him down, covered in soot and weeping because it got away.

It seemed that the numbers had been solving all sorts of difficult mathematical problems that people had been puzzling over for ages. Dame Mildred was very happy about that, and she arranged for her university to pay Brandon to keep on counting down and asking the numbers to do tricks.

Things got a lot better after that. Spring came. Gradually, everyone forgot how angry they'd been with Brandon. He and Elle started school again. Things were getting back to normal.

24

It was the summer holidays. The family were gathered in the living room listening to Brandon count down the last numbers to nothing. Waris was there with them. He'd been there at the beginning and he wanted to be there at the end. Dame Mildred Gosling was there – she wanted to hear it in case the numbers decided to let go of more of their secrets.

And Mr Wyke was there because he was there a lot these days.

'Twenty,' said Brandon.

'Nineteen, eighteen, seventeen, sixteen.'

Everyone held their breaths. What was he going to do next?

'Fifteen,' said Brandon.

'Fourteen,' whispered Elle under her breath.

'Thirteen,' said Brandon.

'Twelve. Go on, Brandon, you can do it. Don't make a mistake now,' said Waris.

'Eleven,' said Brandon.

'Ten,' said Mum. 'Brandon, I'm so proud of you! . . . But please stop counting after this!'

'Nine,' said Brandon.

'Eight,' said Dame Mildred.

'Seven,' said Brandon.
'Six, five, four, three.'

Then he stopped.

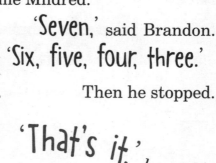

'What?' said Dame Mildred. 'You stopped at three?'

'Yes,' said Brandon.

Elle ran up to him and put her arms around him. 'Thank you, Brandon,' she said. 'That was the nicest thing anyone ever did.'

'But . . . why?' demanded Waris. 'You were almost there!'

'I know,' said Brandon. 'Can we go and have pizza now?'

There was a pause.

'Well, yes, why not?' said Mum. 'A celebration, I suppose.'

'Not for me,' said Dame Mildred. 'I have to go and report back on this to the university. We're going to have to develop a new theory to explain why Brandon stopped at three. I must get to work at once.'

She shook hands with them all, and left. Waris had to leave too – he had a Blog Club meeting that evening. Mr Wyke might have stayed, but Mum decided the celebration should just be for her, Brandon and Elle, to give them a chance to be an ordinary family once more.

At the restaurant, as they waited to be seated, Mum was puzzled.

'Brandon, you counted all the way up to 9,999,999 and then all the way back down to three,' she said. 'But why *three*? Brandon, I love you to pieces, but I will never, ever understand you.'

The waiter came up to see to them.

'How can I help?' he said.

'Table for three, please,' said Mum.

THE END

Howl with laughter with The Bolds

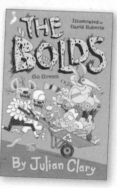

'Wonderful'
Guardian

'Joyful'
Telegraph

'Glorious'
Daily Mail

Spangles McNasty and the Fish of Gold

Steve Webb
Illustrated by Chris Mould

Spangles McNasty is convinced that he can get rich quick by stealing goldfish – after all, aren't they made of solid gold? Together with his friend Sausage-face Pete, he decides to find the great Fish of Gold. Only young Freddie Taylor can stop Spangles' dastardly plan, in a tale full of time-travelling jet skis, madcap chases and haunted custard.

'Unadulterated fun!'
Lovereading

'Ludicrous and funny'
BookTrust

CALLY & JIMMY
TWINS IN TROUBLE

ZOE ANTONIADES
ILLUSTRATED BY **KATIE KEAR**

Cally and Jimmy are twins. Join them in four hilarious
stories as they get into scrapes together, bake some
poisonous cakes, almost ruin their school assembly
and finally have a twintastic birthday party!

'Your kids need this
lovely book'
Kate Beckinsale

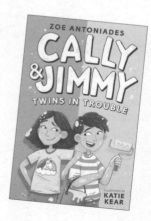

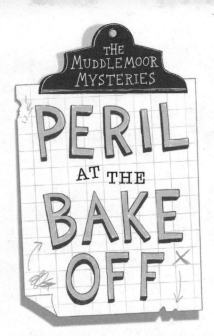

THE MUDDLEMOOR MYSTERIES

PERIL AT THE BAKE OFF

by Ruth Quayle
illustrated by Marta Kissi

It is the summer holiday and Joe Robinson and his cousins are staying with their granny in Muddlemoor village. The problem is . . . Muddlemoor is a hotspot for crime. When Granny's precious cake recipe goes missing days before the Great Village Bake Off, Joe, Tom and Pip are FLABBERGASTED. They KNOW that one of the neighbours has stolen it but the question is, WHO?